WHEN JESUS LAUGHS

Latricia Edwards Scriven, PhD

Latricia Edwards Scriven Publishing, Tallahassee, FL

ISBN: 978-0-9827432-7-0 (Paperback)
ISBN: 978-0-9827432-8-7 (eBook)
ISBN: 978-0-9827432-9-4 (Hardback)
Library of Congress Control Number: 2020911855

Book Cover and Illustrations by macprographics.

Printed in the United States of America.
www.whenjesuslaughs.com

DEDICATION

To **EVERYONE** who desires more laughter and joy, this book is dedicated to **YOU!** May you have as much fun reading it as I had creating it. I hope this makes you want to laugh, giggle, smile, dance, prance, jump, and spin!

Enjoy,

Latricia Edwards
SCRIVEN

WHEN JESUS LAUGHS...

Every day, all around the world,
creation waits to hear
the sound that Jesus makes when he laughs
so we can hurray and hurrah and cheer.

HA
HA
HA
HA
HA
HA

"Laughter is good for the soul," says Jesus.
"And everybody should do it!
So, don't you wait for it to just happen.
Let's hurry up and get to it!"

HA
HA
HA
HA
HA

"Let's laugh, laugh, laugh, 'til our bellies hurt.
And then, let's do it again.
Let's keep on laughing 'til we cannot stop
because that's when the fun will begin."

HA
HA
HA
HA
HA

Now you might be wondering what actually happens
when Jesus starts to laugh and have fun.
Well, hold on tight while I share this story
of Laughing Jesus who is known as God's son.

WHEN JESUS LAUGHS,
stars twinkle and twinkle
as they light up the nighttime sky.

WHEN JESUS LAUGHS,
the butterflies twirl
as they flutter and fly way up high.

WHEN JESUS LAUGHS,
the birds in the air
begin to harmonize as they sing.

WHEN JESUS LAUGHS,
the squirrels in the trees
begin to jump and to bounce and to swing.

WHEN JESUS LAUGHS,
the moon in the sky
starts to dance its own little dance.

WHEN JESUS LAUGHS,
the deer in the bush
run out to strut, and to leap, and to prance.

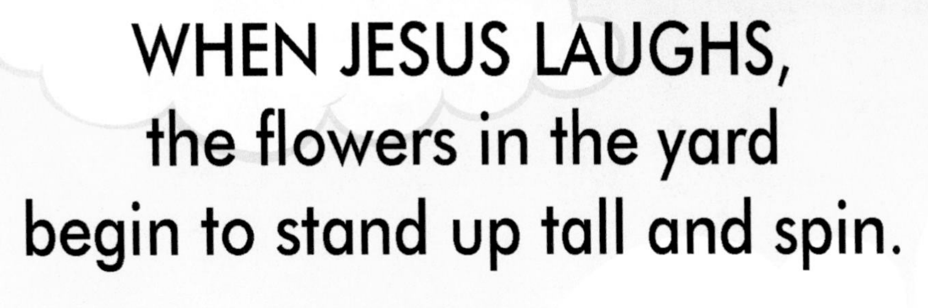

WHEN JESUS LAUGHS,
the flowers in the yard
begin to stand up tall and spin.

WHEN JESUS LAUGHS,
the frogs and giraffes
begin to grin a really big grin.

WHEN JESUS LAUGHS,
the oceans and seas
get excited and start to wave.

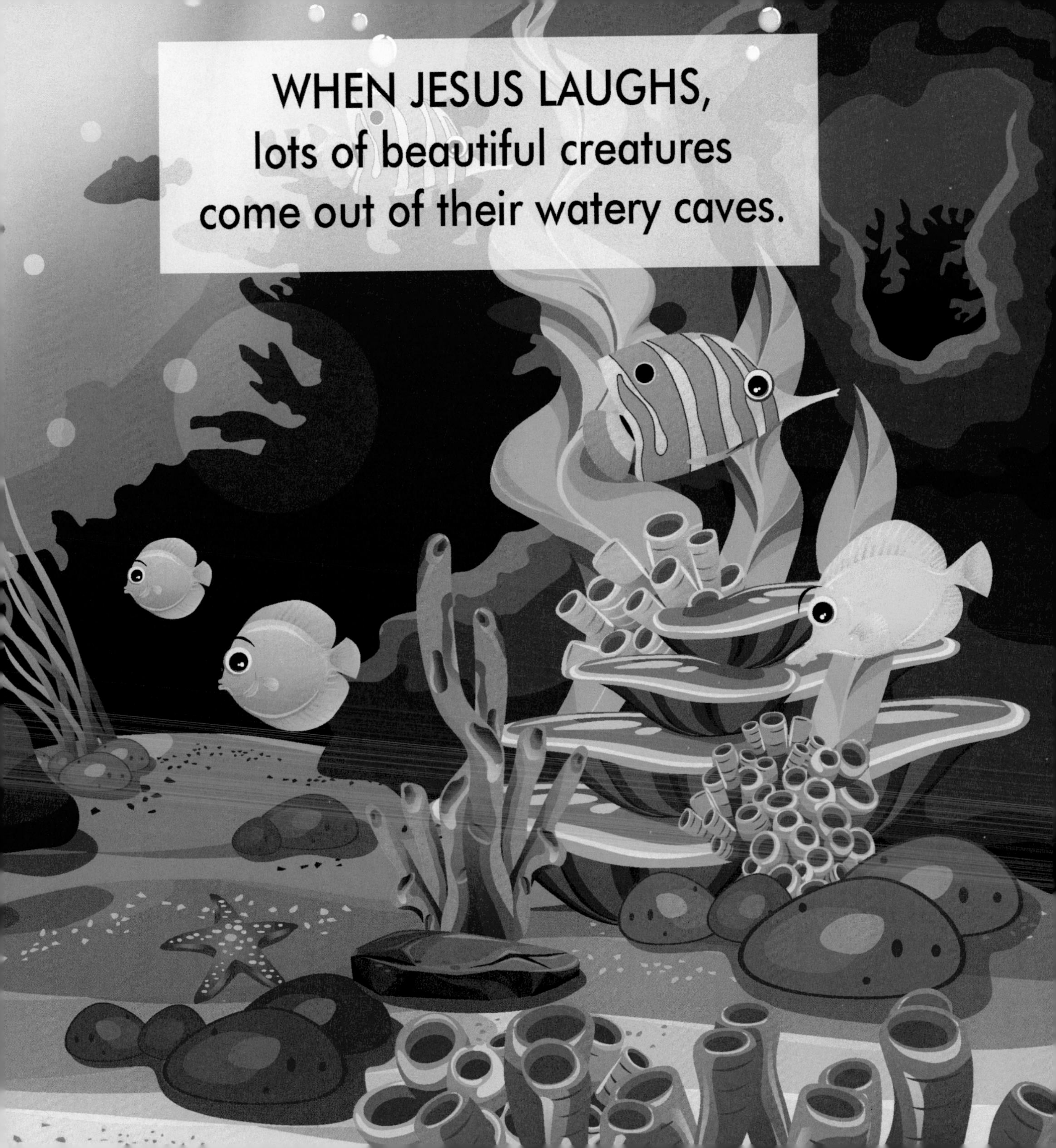
WHEN JESUS LAUGHS,
lots of beautiful creatures
come out of their watery caves.

HA
HA
HA
HA
HA
HA
HA

WHEN JESUS LAUGHS,
He doesn't do it alone.
He invites us all to laugh along too.

HA
HA
HA
HA

WHEN JESUS LAUGHS,
He laughs with all of creation.
And that includes me and you!

A Message from Pastor Latricia

Thank you so much for reading this book! You are **BRILLIANT**, you are **AMAZING**, and you are **LOVED**. Every time you read this book, I hope it brings a smile to your face and makes you want to laugh like Jesus laughs (ha, ha, haha)! Always remember that laughter is a great way to spread happiness and joy in the world. I like to think of laughter as my very own, God-given **SUPERPOWER!** When I'm sad, or down, or discouraged, I always try to find a reason to **LAUGH**. It makes me feel better. Try it and let me know how it works out. Email me anytime at whenjesuslaughs@gmail.com. 😊

Made in the USA
Monee, IL
13 August 2020

38229491R00024